FOR
AXEL & BJORG

First published in 2008 by Orchard Books
First paperback publication in 2009

ORCHARD BOOKS
338 Euston Road, London NW1 3BH
Orchard Books Australia
Level 17/207 Kent St, Sydney, NSW 2000

ISBN 978 1 84616 726 3

Text and illustrations © Shoo Rayner 2008

3 5 7 9 10 8 6 4 2

Printed and bound by CPI Group (UK) Ltd, Croydon, CR0 4YY

Orchard Books is a division of Hachette Children's Books,
an Hachette UK company.

www.hachette.co.uk

VIKING VIK

AND THE BUG HOUSE

SHOO RAYNER

ORCHARD BOOKS

"I'm the bravest!"
Wulf boasted, as he
swung on a rope
over the deep, dark
water of the fiord.

"I'll show you who's got fish brains!"
Wulf snarled. He swung back to the
jetty and leapt on top of Vik,
wrestling him onto the
dusty boards. Vik's
dog, Flek, barked
and snapped at
Wulf's heels.

"Stop it! Stop it!"
Freya shouted.
"Mum's calling us."

The two boys untangled themselves,
growled at each other and sloped off to
see what Mum wanted.

"Take this rubbish to the midden for me," she said. "I can't believe how much mess there is after the Midsummer party."

Two disgusting wastebaskets stood on the ground. They were filled with old bones, fish heads, vegetable peelings, scallop shells and some revolting green scum from the bottom of the cooking pot.

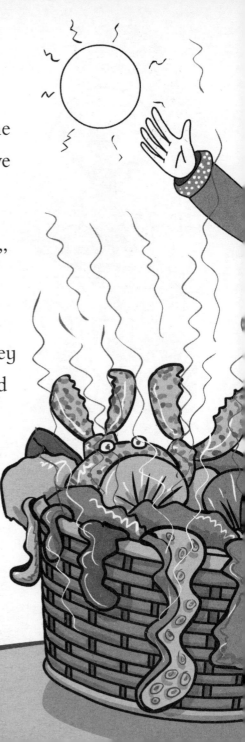

Flek sniffed
the baskets
and wagged
his tail.

Wulf was
about to pick
up the heaviest
basket when he
saw something
squirm in the
smelly mess.

Wulf cleared his throat. "As you think
you're so clever," he told Vik, "you can
carry the heaviest basket." He picked up
the other basket and staggered off
towards the midden.

But Vik had seen the squirming
cockroaches in the basket, too. *Wulf
isn't so brave when it comes to wriggly
things*, he thought.

"Don't go near the old Bug House," Mum called after them. "It's rotten and very dangerous."

MIDSUMMER AND THE MIDNIGHT SUN

On Midsummer's Day in the far north, the sun never sets. It shines all day long and the night is as bright as the day.

The Vikings think this is a reason to have a big party! After all, winter will soon come, when it will be dark and cold all day long.

"This place is revolting!" Vik said, as he tipped the slimy contents of his basket onto the stinking midden. Seagulls screeched around him as they fought for the best bits to eat.

"It really does stink, doesn't it!"
said Freya.

Wulf shuddered. "I hate it here.
There must be hundreds of years
of rubbish. See that brown thing?"
He pointed. "That could be our
great-great-grandfather's poo!"

Wulf tipped his basket onto the steaming pile and skipped away from the mess before anything could wriggle after him.

Vik looked up at the Bug House. "I wonder why it's called the Bug House," he said. "Let's go and have a look."

"Er…Mum said we shouldn't go near it," Wulf said, nervously. "She says it's old and dangerous."

"You're not scared, are you?" Vik winked at Freya.

"Who, me?" Wulf blustered. "I'm scared of nothing!"

Vik, Wulf and Freya
scrambled up the rocky
hillside. "Come on, Flek.
Race you to the top!"
said Vik.

Flek bounded up
the rocks towards the
sinister-looking
building.

THE MIDDEN

The Vikings do not have dustmen to empty the rubbish bins once a week. All the rubbish has to be taken to the midden.

The midden is a piece of land outside the village, where every revolting thing is dumped. It's smelly and slimy and icky and sticky and positively *disgusting*.

The midden is a nice home for rats!

The Bug House was really old. Its wooden walls were bleached by the sun and weathered by the cruel wind that blew up the fiord in the winter.

The ceiling was falling in and the grass roof was covered in weeds.

Freya was worried. "Let's go back!
Mum told us not to come here."

The two boys ignored her. They
climbed the creaking steps and peered
into the dark doorway.

"Why don't you?" said Vik.

"I said it first," argued Wulf.

"You're not scared, are you?" Vik grinned.

"Not me!"
Wulf snarled.
He sprang down
from the steps,
picked up a stick
and threw it into
the Bug House.

"Yap!" Flek thought Wulf
was playing a game. He
bounded through the doorway
and chased after the stick.

Vik looked on
in horror. "Flek!
Come back!"

The sound of old, rotten floorboards creaking and breaking echoed around the hillside. Then Flek began to howl.

"It sounds like he's hurt himself," said Freya.

"I'm coming to get you, Flek!" Vik called. Without thinking, he crept through the doorway into the dark, cavernous building.

YOWWWLL

Vik soon understood why it was called the Bug House. Small things skittered and scuttled in the darkness. A faint light came from the floor in the direction of Flek's pathetic whimpering.

"Argh!" Something small and flappy flew at Vik's head. Vik batted the creature away as it tried to crawl into his ear.

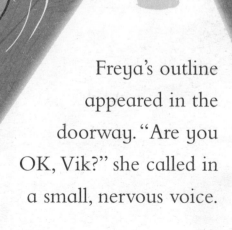

Freya's outline appeared in the doorway. "Are you OK, Vik?" she called in a small, nervous voice.

"I'm all right," said Vik. "I think it was a bat." He took another step and found himself tangled in a huge spider's web. The sticky strands covered his head. Vik felt hairy legs crawl over his face. He tore at the web and spat the sticky stuff out of his mouth.

"Bleugh!" he shivered. He could hear Wulf laughing outside.

"I'll show him," Vik muttered.

To make himself feel brave,
Vik thought about the great god,
Thor – *he* wouldn't be scared.

This is easy compared to the tests Thor had to go through, Vik thought, as something small and furry scuttled over his feet.

"Wahh!" Vik leapt in the air. His foot crashed through the rotten floor.

"Careful, Vik!" Freya called.

Suddenly, with an enormous creak and a crash of splitting wood, the floor gave way and there was Flek. He had fallen through the rotten floor, too. He was trapped between the wooden floor and the ground under the Bug House. Flek's collar was caught on a splinter of wood. He couldn't move.

Vik grabbed the frightened dog
and gently unhooked him.

"There you are," said Vik, hugging his
faithful friend. Flek wagged his tail and
licked Vik's face as if he'd never met
anyone so wonderful before.

THE TRIALS OF THOR

Thor's greatest trial was with the Midgard Serpent. Thor caught the serpent when he was fishing.

They fought together for a long time, but the serpent escaped.

Thor is destined to catch the Midgard serpent before the world ends on the day of Ragnarok.

The hole in the floor was big enough for Vik to see Wulf outside the Bug House. He was dancing around, holding his sides with laughter.

"Ha! Ha! Don't forget to bring the stick back, will you, Vik?" he chortled. "There's a good doggy!"

"I'll show him," Vik whispered to Flek.

"Are you all right, Vik?" Freya called from the doorway. "Speak to me!"

Vik said nothing. His eyes were used to the darkness now. As he crept towards the door, he could see beetles and woodlice crawling on the floor. He picked some up and held them in one hand.

A large spider scurried in front of him. He grabbed it by one of its long, hairy legs.

"Quick, Wulf!" Freya called. "I think
Vik's hurt. He's not answering me."

"All right, all right," Wulf complained.
"I suppose I'll have to save him."

Vik was ready for him. When Wulf
loomed through the doorway, Vik tossed
the bugs at him.

"Ee-e-e-k!" Wulf screamed like
a little girl. He tumbled backwards,
batting the creatures from his face with
his hands.

"Get them off me!" he cried, as he tripped and stumbled down the Bug House steps.

"Argh! I hate spiders," he yelled, as he slid down the rocky hillside.

"Urgh!" he squealed, as he landed – *splat!* – in the middle of the stinky midden. Mice and rats scurried away and a flock of angry seagulls shot up into the air.

Vik and Freya scrambled down the rocks to help Wulf. "I thought you said you were the bravest!" laughed Vik, helping Wulf to his feet. "You're not scared of a few little bugs and spiders, are you?"

Wulf was covered in disgusting slop. Flek sniffed him with great interest.

"Urgh!" Freya pointed at Wulf's head. "What is *that*?"

Vik couldn't stop laughing. A large
fish skeleton lay draped over Wulf's hat.
Its glassy eyes bulged and stared.

Wulf shook his fists and stamped his feet. "Raaargh!" he yelled with rage, as he ran to the water's edge, dived fully clothed into the fiord and began washing off the filthy mess.

"I was right," Vik giggled. "Wulf really does have fish brains after all!"

SHOO RAYNER

Viking Vik and the Wolves	978 1 84616 725 6
Viking Vik and the Big Fight	978 1 84616 731 7
Viking Vik and the Chariot Race	978 1 84616 730 0
Viking Vik and the Trolls	978 1 84616 724 9
Viking Vik and the Bug House	978 1 84616 726 3
Viking Vik and the Lucky Stone	978 1 84616 727 0
Viking Vik and the Longship	978 1 84616 728 7
Viking Vik and the Secret Shield	978 1 84616 729 4

All priced at £4.99

The Viking Vik stories are available from all good bookshops,
or can be ordered direct from the publisher:
Orchard Books, PO BOX 29, Douglas IM99 1BQ
Credit card orders please telephone 01624 836000
or fax 01624 837033 or visit our internet site: www.orchardbooks.co.uk
or e-mail: bookshop@enterprise.net for details.

To order please quote title, author and ISBN
and your full name and address.
Cheques and postal orders should be made payable to 'Bookpost plc.'
Postage and packing is FREE within the UK
(overseas customers should add £2.00 per book).

Prices and availability are subject to change.